SCHOOL
ICE BREAKER

Tom & Tony Bradman

Illustrated by Si Clark

A & C Black • London

D0543806

3 8028 02192852 0

www.acblack.com

Text copyright © 2011 Tony Bradman and Tom Bradman
Illustrations copyright © 2011 Si Clark

The rights of Tony Bradman, Tom Bradman and Si Clark to be
identified as the authors and illustrator of this work have been
asserted by them in accordance with the Copyrights,
Designs and Patents Act 1988.

ISBN 978-1-4081-2378-2

A CIP catalogue for this book is available from the British Library.

All rights reserved. No part of this publication may be
reproduced in any form or by any means – graphic, electronic
or mechanical, including photocopying, recording, taping or
information storage and retrieval systems – without
the prior permission in writing of the publishers.

This book is produced using paper that is made from wood
grown in managed, sustainable forests. It is natural, renewable and
recyclable. The logging and manufacturing processes conform
to the environmental regulations of the country of origin.

Printed and bound in Great Britain
by CPI Cox & Wyman, Reading, RG1 8EX.

CHAPTER ONE
ICE PLANET

'Whoa, check it out!' said Luke as the shuttle came in low over the planet's surface. He was looking through the viewport next to his seat and just couldn't stop grinning. 'I've never seen this much snow... this is going to be so cool!'

Dazzling whiteness stretched away as far as he could see, snow covering the uneven ground, making it look like a giant rumpled duvet. In the distance stood a mountain range, great rocky peaks rising above huge, glittering glaciers. The shuttle itself was crowded, the seats occupied by the thirty kids of Primary One, Luke's class,

all of them wearing thick hooded coats and sturdy snow boots.

Their teacher Clarke was at the controls. He was a hologram, a perfect replica of Albert Einstein, complete with wild white hair and a droopy moustache.

'I don't know about cool,' muttered Luke's friend Yasmin. She shivered as she peered

over Luke's shoulder, a frown on her brown face, her jet-black hair pulled back tightly in a ponytail. 'I'll bet it's absolutely freezing down there.'

'It'll be cold all right,' said Yuri, the flame-haired and freckled member of the trio. He was sitting in the last seat of their row. 'But it won't be *absolutely* freezing. Absolute zero is defined as being minus 273 degrees Centigrade – '

'Er... thanks for the scientific heads-up, Yuri,' Yasmin said quickly, before he could really get into full geek-lecture-mode. 'I'm just glad I put on plenty of layers. In fact I'd much rather have stayed put in our nice warm spaceship.'

'Well, I wouldn't,' said Luke. 'I can't wait to land and have some fun.'

Luke was tired of living on a spaceship, however warm it was. He and his

schoolmates and their families had been stuck on the *Buzz Aldrin* for ages. They had escaped from a terminally polluted Earth and were in search of a new home somewhere else in the galaxy. But so far they had found nothing except barren worlds they could never live on, and hostile aliens of one kind or another.

Then a few days ago they had come across a new star system with several planets circling its weak sun. Luke's mum was Captain Riley, commander of the *Buzz Aldrin*, so he knew the ship's science team had scanned the planets. The results had been mostly disappointing. Only one was capable of supporting life, but it was too cold to make a decent home for the remnants of humanity.

Everyone on the *Buzz* had been very glum – until Luke had his brainwave. He

had asked his mum if they could spend some time on the ice planet – a few days of winter sports and fun would do them all a lot of good. Mum had agreed it was a great idea, and said the science team could also set up a research station to investigate some rather strange readings the scanners had picked up.

A rota had been organised, and today it was Primary One's turn to fly down in the shuttle from the *Buzz* to the planet. Now their flight was nearly over.

'Check your seatbelts, everybody!' said Clarke. 'We're about to land.'

Luke just had time to glimpse the purple domes of the research station before the shuttle's thrusters started kicking up a cloud of snow. Seconds later there was a slight bump as they touched down. Clarke switched off the thrusters and opened

the rear door while the kids unbuckled their seatbelts. Soon they were streaming off the ramp and onto the surface, Luke, Yasmin and Yuri in the lead.

The friends skidded to a halt and stood for a moment gazing at the scene in front of them. Luke closed his eyes and breathed in the cold, sharp air, so unlike the awful, endlessly recycled stuff they had to put up with on the *Buzz Aldrin*.

Suddenly something very cold and wet smacked straight into his face. He wiped his eyes and saw Yasmin grinning at him, another snowball in her hand.

'Score one for me!' she said. 'Maybe it's not so bad down here after all.'

'Right, you asked for it!' said Luke, laughing. He scooped some snow into a big ball and threw it at her as hard as he could. Yasmin ducked, and threw the

snowball she was holding at him. Yuri laughed too and pelted both of them, and of course the rest of the class joined in, chucking snowballs at them and each other. Everyone was having a terrific time – everyone except Clarke.

'Children, behave yourselves!' he shouted, his head fizzing as a snowball passed through it. 'There will be plenty of time for games later. We're supposed to check in at the research station first and hear how the science team is doing.'

'No thanks!' yelled Yasmin. 'This is fun – and that sounds really boring!'

'Speak for yourself, Yasmin,' said Yuri. 'I'd like to talk to them, actually.'

'You won't be doing much talking once I hit you with this,' Luke yelled. He had put together a monster snowball, and now he threw it. But Yasmin jogged his arm and

it missed Yuri by a long way. It flew over the red-haired boy's head... and smacked into the face of a man who had appeared behind him.

'Whoops!' said Luke, and laughed. But the man looked very cross indeed.

CHAPTER TWO
NASTY MEN

The man was big and ugly. He had a broken nose and the cold, cruel eyes of a snake, and he was wearing a strange outfit – a greasy old baseball cap and a long grey coat, his chest criss-crossed with ammunition belts full of cartridges. They were obviously for the rifle he carried slung on its strap over his shoulder.

Luke saw that the man had a couple of mean-looking friends with him – a pair of smaller men, one totally bald, the other's face covered in a thick black beard. Both were dressed in much the same way as the first man, both carried rifles – and

both were scowling. Luke gulped, and took a step backwards.

'Er... that wasn't meant for you,' he said, his voice squeaky. 'Sorry.'

'You will be, sonny,' snarled the man, angrily wiping the snow from his face. But he glanced over at Clarke and seemed to change his mind about whatever he'd been thinking of doing. 'Come on, lads,' he muttered. 'Let's leave these brats to their stupid games.'

He turned on his heel and headed for a small, tracked vehicle parked nearby. His friends gave Luke one last nasty look, then scurried off as well. The three men climbed into the car and it rumbled away, crushing the snow beneath its tracks, dirty black smoke pouring out of its exhaust.

'Who the heck was that?' said Yuri. 'He was like a bad guy in a movie.'

'That's probably what he wants to be,' snorted Yasmin. 'His name is Quint. The bald one is called Leon, and the one with the big beard is called Biff.'

'Oh, so that's Quint!' said Luke. 'I heard my mum talking about him the other day. As far as I can make out, she doesn't think he's a very nice person.'

'You can say that again,' muttered Yasmin. 'I've heard lots of bad stories about him – he's a real troublemaker. And where did they get those guns?'

'They're hunters,' said Luke, remembering something he'd heard his mum say. 'Or at least they'd like to be. They must have brought the guns and that filthy old car from Earth.'

'Well, I certainly hope they don't find anything to hunt here,' said Yasmin. 'I hate the idea of nasty men like that killing

defenceless animals.'

'Hear hear,' said Yuri, nodding seriously. 'I'm with you on that, Yasmin.'

'Me too,' said Luke, scooping up some snow. 'Now, back to having fun.'

'Er, I don't think so,' said Yasmin. 'Clarke is rounding everyone up.'

Yasmin was right. Clarke had got the rest of the class under control, and soon he was marching them away from the shuttle and towards the purple domes.

Their visit to the research station turned out to be interesting – for Yuri. The science team was in the largest dome and was led by the *Buzz Aldrin*'s elderly chief engineer, Asimov. He was happy to explain to the children what they were doing, and waved his long, thin arms around as he showed them all the bleeping machines they had set up, his hair even wilder than Clarke's.

'So have you found out anything more about those strange readings, Mr Asimov?' said Yuri. Yasmin nudged Luke and rolled her eyes. Luke smiled.

'Excellent question, young man,' said Mr Asimov. 'We're pretty sure they're coming from something organic, but we don't know exactly what. Now, if you just follow me I'll show you the fascinating rock samples we've collected...'

Asimov headed to the other side of the dome, Clarke and most of the class trailing

behind him. Yasmin pulled a face and hung back, and Luke did too. He had seen Chung, Mum's second-in-command, and wanted to talk to her.

'Hi, you two!' she said, smiling at Luke and Yasmin, pushing back her dark hair. In front of her was a screen showing the area behind the dome where the science team's hover-jeep was parked. 'Not interested in rock samples?'

Yasmin and Luke laughed, and they talked for a while. Chung told them she had already been skiing, and that the nearest hills were great for snowboarding.

'Sounds good,' said Luke. 'But I hope we don't bump into Quint and his pals anywhere. I don't understand why Mum let them come down here at all.'

'She couldn't really stop them, Luke,' said Chung with a shrug. 'I suppose they've

got as much right as anyone else on the *Buzz* to get some fresh air.'

'They haven't got the right to go round killing living creatures,' said Yasmin. 'Guns are evil, and I don't think they should have been allowed to bring them.'

'Don't worry about it too much, Yasmin,' said Chung. 'If you ask me they're all talk. Besides, we haven't yet found any living creatures they could shoot.'

Yasmin was about to say something else, but then the metal floor beneath their feet started to shake. Luke and Yasmin looked at each other in alarm.

'Hey, what's with the tremors?' Luke said nervously. 'Is it an earthquake?'

'We don't think so,' said Chung, frowning. 'But that's the third time today.'

Luke felt uneasy. Maybe there was more to this planet than met the eye.

CHAPTER THREE
ALIEN EYES

The shaking stopped as suddenly as it had begun, much to Luke's relief. It did have one good result, though. Asimov announced that Primary One's tour of the research station was over, as the science team had to analyse what had happened.

'At last!' said Yasmin. 'Please sir, can we just go and have some fun now?'

'Yes, Yasmin, of course,' said Clarke, giving her an indulgent smile. 'I'd like to say a couple of things about safety before you head off, though. Kids, wait!'

It was too late. The whole class stampeded out of the dome, even Yuri,

with Luke and Yasmin in the lead. Within minutes the three friends were trudging through the snow, making for the nearby hills Chung had said were good for snowboarding. They kept up a snowball fight along the way, Yasmin proving to be the most powerful and accurate shot, the boys having to work together to have any chance of beating her. After a while they reached the top of a hill.

Chung had lent them her snowboard, and Yasmin decided she should have the first go. She was pretty good too, flying down the steep slope, Luke and Yuri

whooping their encouragement. She made a perfect stop, curving round and sending out a spray of snow like a surfer on a wave. Then she came running back up the hill and threw the board onto the snow in front of Luke and Yuri.

'Who's going next?' she said, panting. 'Bet neither of you can do better.'

'Er... I wouldn't argue with that,' said Yuri. 'So you can count me out. I'm more comfortable with my laptop than with one of those. Over to you, Luke.'

'No problem,' Luke said, trying to sound confident even though he felt quite nervous. He wasn't going to let Yasmin – a *girl* – get one over him. 'OK, then,' he murmured, stepping onto the snowboard and pushing off. 'GERONIMO!'

He moved quite slowly to begin with, but soon he was whizzing down the slope, his

cheeks burning as he sliced through the freezing air. It was fantastic, a really great sensation, and he couldn't help grinning. Yuri was cheering him on, then yelling something about watching out for the huge rock at the bottom of the slope. Suddenly Luke's grin vanished – he didn't know how to stop!

The rock was getting closer, looming in front of him, so Luke did the only thing possible – he dived off the snowboard, landing head first in the snow, rolling over and over until he finally came to a halt. He lay groaning, surprised he was still alive, his top half buried in a snow drift that seemed to be moving.

Luke quickly raised his head, worried he might have started an avalanche – only to find himself being stared at by a pair of unblinking, very alien eyes.

They belonged to a chunky, foot-long, millipede-like creature with a ridged grey hide and dozens of tiny legs. For a brief instant alien and human continued to stare at each other – and then the creature started moving towards him. Luke squeaked in panic and struggled to free himself completely from the snow, but ended up on his back – and watched horrified as the creature flowed onto his

chest. It opened a wide mouth, revealing a set of sharp-looking teeth.

Fear paralysed Luke's limbs and he closed his eyes, terrified of what the creature was about to do. Then he felt something rough and wet on his cheek.

'Awww, I think it likes you!' he heard Yasmin say. 'How cool is that?'

Luke opened his eyes and saw that the creature was licking his face with a long, green tongue. He sat up and tried to push it off, but it was harder to shift than an eager puppy, and soon his face was dripping with alien creature spit. Yasmin and Yuri were standing over him, Yasmin with a soppy look on her face, Yuri making notes on the laptop he'd whipped out of his backpack.

'Well, don't just stand there, you two,' said Luke. 'Get this thing off me!'

'It's not a thing, Luke Riley, it's a living

creature,' snapped Yasmin, glaring at him. 'You could have killed the poor animal landing on top of it like that.' But then she smiled. 'Mind you, the way you dived off was pretty funny... '

'Too right,' said Yuri, and they both laughed. 'You looked ridiculous!'

Luke got to his feet and wiped his face, scowling. But he couldn't keep it up for long – he was already starting to like the

friendly little alien creature. It was rubbing its chunky body against his legs now, purring and making soft yip-yip noises. He couldn't imagine it ever being threatening or hurting anybody.

'You two can laugh all you like,' said Luke with a shrug. 'But I'm the one who'll go down in history as the boy who discovered life on this planet.'

'Not if we get to the research station first, you won't!' laughed Yasmin.

She ran off, Yuri laughing and following, the creature flowing away after them. Luke sighed and picked up the snowboard. But he paused, sure he had seen the huge rock moving slightly. Then he shook his head, and trudged on.

Behind him the grey, ridged rock moved again, like something uncoiling...

CHAPTER FOUR
A NICE TROPHY

On the walk back to the research station Yasmin decided the alien was female, and named her Milly because she resembled a huge millipede. Luke and Yuri liked the name, and they also liked the way Milly scampered along beside them making her little yip-yip noises. In fact they were all having such a good time they burst into the research station laughing, and almost fell over each other.

'Whoa, cool your jets, kids!' said Chung, holding up her hands. 'We've got a lot of delicate equipment in here...' Then her eyes grew wide as she noticed the strange

creature peering from behind Yasmin's legs. 'What in space is that?'

'A completely new life-form!' said Yuri, grinning. 'We discovered her in – '

'What do you mean, *we*?' said Luke indignantly. 'I'm the one who found her.'

'Crashed into her, more like,' Yasmin said, bending down to stroke the little creature. 'She's called Milly and she's really cute. Can we keep her, Chung?'

'I don't know about that,' said Chung. 'We'd better let Asimov and his team have a look at her first, just to be on the safe side. Come on, they're over here.'

Chung headed to another part of the dome and the kids went with her. Milly, however, insisted on stopping to examine almost everything she saw. In the end Luke had the clever idea of tempting her to keep moving with one of the high-energy

snack bars Mum had put in his backpack. It immediately did the trick, Milly following the treat obediently and gobbling it up with obvious pleasure.

Asimov was running scans of the planet's weather, but the engineer quickly turned his attention to Milly. Soon he was putting her through a whole series of tests. She wasn't too keen on his machines with their bleeping and flashing lights, and Luke had to bribe her with more energy bars to stay put. But he really liked the way she nuzzled at his hand when he gave one to her.

'Fascinating,' said Asimov at last, peering at Milly. She was sitting on the table in front of him, happily demolishing another energy bar. 'I'd say she's in the opening stages of a metamorphosis.' Clarke and Yuri nodded but Luke, Yasmin and Chung looked blank. 'Changing, like caterpillars into butterflies,'

Asimov added. 'And as with that kind of life-cycle back on Earth, she could turn into something very different. Still, we're fairly sure she's harmless.'

'That's all I need to hear,' said Chung. 'OK, kids, you can keep her for now.'

The three friends grinned at each other. But before they could say anything they heard the sound of heavy boots. Luke looked round and saw that Quint and his cronies had entered the dome. They were advancing on the science team's area, their faces even grimmer than before, their rifles pointing at Milly!

Luke went cold all over and grabbed the small creature from the table. Milly must have sensed his fear for her – she instantly coiled into a tight ball, making herself as small as possible. Chung leapt forward to stand between the children and the men,

her hands raised. 'Hey, what do you think you're doing?' she said.

'We're just trying to protect everyone, that's all,' Quint growled, reluctantly lowering his weapon. 'That there alien could be a pretty dangerous beast...'

'Well, you're wrong!' yelled Luke. 'The science team say she's harmless.'

'Oh, it's a she, is it?' said Quint, laughing. Leon and Biff smirked. 'Ah, how sweet, the brats have got themselves a little pet! Well,

at least we know now there's something we can hunt on this poor excuse for a planet.'

'What do you mean?' said Yasmin. 'She's the only life-form we've found.'

'Well, she must have a few relatives around here somewhere,' said Quint, shrugging. 'I'll bet your little pet has got parents and quite a few brothers and sisters. Don't worry, though – we'll bring you a nice trophy or two to cry over.'

'But... but... you can't do that!' spluttered Yasmin, outraged. 'It's not right.'

'So who's going to stop us – brats like you?' sneered Quint. 'Besides, it's what our species is all about – humans have been hunters since long before the Stone Age. Now we travel vast distances, discover new planets, find new life-forms – and kill them!' Quint laughed, and the men high-fived each other.

'It's people like you who ruined Earth,' muttered Luke, hardly able to believe what he was hearing. He was glad Milly couldn't understand what Quint was saying, although she had begun to wriggle against his chest almost as if she did.

'OK, Mr Quint,' said Chung. 'This is a restricted area, and I'm going to have to ask you to leave. I'll also be speaking to Captain Riley about the way you – '

She was interrupted by a deep rumbling sound that seemed to come from beneath the dome. The floor shook, and a huge bulge suddenly appeared in it, knocking over Asimov's table, sending all his delicate equipment flying.

Luke staggered, holding on to Milly. But she had suddenly gone very still.

CHAPTER FIVE
GREEN SLIME

Soon the whole dome was shaking. There was a horrendous screeching noise as the struts holding it up began to twist and buckle, and then a large equipment locker toppled over with a CRASH! 'Quick, everybody outside!' yelled Chung.

She hustled Luke, Yasmin and Yuri towards the door, Asimov and his team following. Chung didn't let any of them stop until she thought they were all a safe distance from the dome. Luke saw Quint, Leon and Biff nearby, and Clarke leading the rest of Primary One out of another dome, the children looking scared. The

ground was shaking even more, and the rumbling noise was getting louder.

'I'm beginning to think I don't like this planet after all,' said Yasmin.

'Me too,' said Luke. 'This tremor is definitely worse than last time.'

'It's interesting, though,' said Yuri. 'The movement seems localised...'

'Hold on a second, brain-box,' said Yasmin. 'What in space is that?'

Yasmin was pointing at the frozen, snow-covered ground next to the research team's dome. A new bulge had appeared there, one that grew and grew, the icy ground breaking and cracking, the rumbling almost ear-splitting now. At last something enormous burst into sight, a giant worm, like an immense living train, its long body dark grey and ridged, its eyes bigger than footballs.

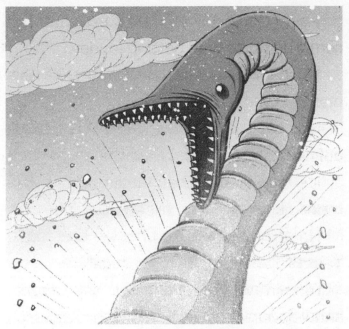

The creature rose into the air, opening its mouth to reveal enormous, pointed teeth, and swooped down on the dome, biting a great chunk out of it, chewing and crunching the metal outer shell and spitting bits out. After a moment it turned its gaze on the humans, whose own mouths were wide open with shock. And then it dropped

to the ground and headed towards them at incredible speed.

'RUN!' yelled Chung, and they all fled, most of them screaming in panic.

Luke ran with the rest, Milly in his arms, but he hadn't got very far when he tripped over a rock and fell headlong into the snow. He rolled onto his back, still holding Milly tightly against his chest – and found himself looking up at the most terrifying sight he had ever seen, the giant worm looming above him.

Hot, foul-smelling breath wafted from the creature's mouth, and green slime dripped onto him from the worm's nostrils. The beast slowly lowered its face until it was almost close enough for Luke to touch, and for a moment he was utterly convinced it was about to gobble him up. Then he saw its eyes were fixed on Milly,

and he began to worry that it was her the worm was after.

Milly, however, didn't seem worried. In fact she was looking straight back at the worm and making lots of those yip-yip noises. The worm moved its head from side to side – then turned and plunged into the snow, its whole incredible grey length disappearing like a whale diving deep in the sea, a trail of cracks in the icy ground marking its passage as it rumbled off towards the mountains.

Luke let out a breath he hadn't known he was holding, and looked down at Milly, who was purring now. There had been something strange about what had just happened. It had almost seemed as if Milly had spoken with the worm...

'Are you OK, Luke?' said Yasmin, running over to him with Yuri. 'I was going to save

you till I saw all that alien, er… snot. Not good for the hair.'

'I'm fine, thanks,' said Luke. 'And obviously your hair must come first.'

'But what an amazing creature!' said Yuri. 'It's absolutely magnificent!'

'You got that right,' said a voice behind the three friends. 'It looks as if there might be something worth hunting on this frozen lump of space rock after all.'

Luke whipped round and saw that Quint had come over with Leon and Biff. It had been Quint who had spoken, and all three men were smirking.

'You cannot be serious,' snarled Yasmin. 'It will eat you for breakfast.'

'I think we'll be the ones doing the eating, if it tastes any good,' laughed Quint. 'It's only the size of a whale, and humans didn't have any trouble hunting whales on Earth,

did they? Right lads, we've got a trail to follow.'

Quint led his two henchmen to their vehicle, and soon it roared off in a cloud of black smoke, heading in the same direction as the giant worm, towards the mountains. Milly squirmed in Luke's arms, and had long since stopped purring. She was making a sad little noise instead, a kind of unhappy, low moaning.

'I know, Milly,' said Luke, softly stroking her. 'We don't like them either.'

'Huh, that's putting it mildly,' muttered Yasmin. 'I hope they do get eaten.'

'But what if they don't?' said Yuri, his face full of concern. 'What if they track that incredible creature and...' He stopped speaking, unable to carry on.

'We can't let that happen,' said Luke. 'We've got to stop them, somehow. Come on, let's go and ask Chung if we can get in touch with my mum.'

He heard a deep rumble in the distance as he spoke, and felt a faint tremor beneath his feet.

CHAPTER SIX
A STORM COMING

They didn't have to go and find Chung, however – the *Buzz Aldrin*'s second-in-command found them instead. She had seen Luke fall in front of the worm, but she had fallen at the same time, tripping over another rock in all the panic and getting stuck in a deep snowdrift. It had taken her a while to dig herself out.

'I'm so relieved you're OK, Luke!' she said. 'And of course you must talk to your mum. I need to speak to her as well, let her know what just happened.'

'At least we know now what the strange readings were,' said Yuri. 'I'll bet the

scanners were picking up the movements of those worms underground.'

'Good thinking, Yuri,' said Chung. 'We'll have to see what Asimov says.'

Asimov had already come to the same conclusion, although he was having a lot of trouble confirming it – most of the science team's stuff had been destroyed or badly damaged in the giant worm's attack on the dome. But they did manage to salvage enough radio equipment for Chung to report to Captain Riley. Then Luke spoke to his mum and told her about Quint's intentions.

'You have to stop them, Mum,' said Luke. The screen in front of him showed Mum's face. She was on the bridge of the *Buzz*, crew members at consoles in the background. Even though the screen crackled and fizzed with interference, Luke

could tell she was worried. 'There must be something you can do.'

'I'm sorry, Luke,' said Mum. 'There isn't really, not at the moment, anyway. Besides, I'm more worried about everybody's safety down there. Of course I don't want Quint to kill that creature, but it does sound pretty dangerous. And if Yuri is right, the readings could mean that there are plenty more under the ice.'

'You mean, like a herd of those things?' said Yasmin. Yuri glanced at her, his eyebrows raised. 'What?' she said. 'I watch nature programmes too.'

'But there's another problem,' said Luke's mum. 'We've analysed the weather scans Asimov sent earlier, and we think there's a storm coming in your direction, a big one. I want you kids off the planet and back on the *Buzz* long before it hits. You'd better tell Clarke I need a word with him. See you soon.'

The friends walked off a little further behind the destroyed dome so they could talk privately, Milly scampering at their feet. Yasmin was not happy.

'Grrr... typical grown-ups!' she growled. 'No offence, Luke. But we can't let Quint get away with it. I'll never, ever forgive myself if he kills that creature.'

'Neither will I,' said Luke. 'Especially as it might be Milly's mum or dad.'

Yasmin and Yuri looked at him and then at the little alien, their eyes wide and mouths open. Milly was making sad noises, and Luke picked her up.

'Whoa, brain overload!' said Yasmin at last. 'How did you work that out?'

'But it's obvious, Yasmin!' said Yuri before Luke could reply. 'I should have seen it myself. The grey ridged skin, being in the early stages of a change...'

'Exactly,' said Luke. 'But it was only when I saw the two of them together that I realised how much they looked like each other. And it was Milly the big one was interested in, not us. I'm sure Milly was talking to it somehow, too.'

It took a while for the boys to convince Yasmin. Yuri pointed out that in most

species on Earth the young were small and grew into something much bigger, and that Milly wouldn't need her legs once she was the size of the giant worm.

'OK, OK, enough of the geeky stuff already!' said Yasmin eventually. 'I'll take your word for it. The question is – what are we actually going to do?'

'We'll just have to stop Quint ourselves,' said Luke with a shrug.

'Oh yeah?' said Yasmin. 'We don't even know where they are.'

'I can track them on my laptop,' said Yuri. 'I've got a special app.'

'We'll never catch them,' said Yasmin. 'They've got a big head start.'

'You're right,' said Luke. Then his eyes fell on the vehicle parked nearby. 'Hey, what if we used the science team's hover car? It's pretty fast, isn't it?'

'Definitely!' said Yuri, grinning. 'It's a lot faster than Quint's old banger.'

'So, let me get this straight, Luke,' said Yasmin. 'You're suggesting we steal the hover-jeep, drive across an alien planet in the middle of a huge snowstorm instead of going back to the *Buzz Aldrin* as we've been

told to by your scary mum, and confront a bunch of killers with guns. What happens then?'

'We'll work something out,' said Luke, grinning at her. 'We always do.'

Yasmin scowled at her friends for a moment. Then she grinned too.

'Count me in,' she said. 'On one condition, though – I get to drive the hover-jeep. Girls are better drivers than boys, it's been scientifically proved.'

'No problem,' said Luke before Yuri could start arguing with her. The sky was darkening and they didn't have any time to waste. 'Let's get going.'

CHAPTER SEVEN
REAL DANGER

There wasn't much room inside the hover-jeep. The three friends were squeezed together on its single bench seat – Yasmin in the middle at the controls, Yuri to her left with his laptop open, and Luke to her right, with a restless Milly on his lap. They were skimming quickly through a snowy waste, more snow swirling in the air around them, a strong wind buffeting the hover-jeep every so often.

'How much further, Yuri?' said Yasmin. 'We're almost in the mountains.'

'Not far,' said Yuri. Luke could see a detailed map on the laptop's screen, and

guessed that the hover-jeep was the blue dot moving swiftly across it. The stationary red dot it was heading for had to be Quint's vehicle. 'They don't seem to be moving,' added Yuri. 'We should be able to spot them quite soon.'

'Huh, you'll be lucky,' muttered Yasmin, frowning. 'I can hardly make out anything in this snow. But hey, hold on a second... what's that over there?'

Directly ahead was a slope with enormous rocks poking up through the deep snow. Luke could see a dark, square shape at the foot of the biggest boulder.

'Yes, it's them!' said Yuri, excited. 'I'd recognise that old banger anywhere.'

'They're not much good at parking, are they?' said Luke. He realised the vehicle must have crashed into the rock. One of the tracks had come off and its front end

was totally smashed. 'I suppose we'd better find out if they're OK.'

'You are joking, aren't you?' said Yasmin. 'I hope they're frozen solid.'

'No problem!' said Luke. 'You stay here while us boys bravely rescue some grown-ups. I mean, you don't want your hair to get frizzy or anything, do you?'

'Very funny,' snapped Yasmin. 'Go on, then. The things I do for you two...'

Luke and Yuri grinned at each other, but their grins vanished when Yasmin opened the doors. The icy wind instantly leapt into the hover-jeep like some frantic beast, swirling and whirling and filling the interior with snowflakes. The friends climbed out, pulling their hoods tightly round their faces, and trudged over to the big boulder. Milly scampered ahead, not bothered by the weather.

'They're not here!' said Yasmin, peering into the vehicle and yelling to make herself heard above the wailing of the wind. 'Maybe they started walking...'

'But why walk when you can ride?' yelled somebody else. 'Hello, brats.'

Luke whipped round and saw Quint, Leon and Biff emerging from behind the boulder. The men took up a position between the hover-jeep and the kids, and stood facing them. 'Looks like we got here just in time, Quint,' said Luke, pointing at the hunter's broken vehicle. 'Did you run into some trouble?'

'Nothing major,' said the big man, smirking at the children. 'Just a mishap. It looks like we'll be all right now though, eh lads?' His two friends laughed.

It suddenly occurred to Luke that he and his own friends were in real danger.

He'd gone up against alien armadas and psychotic super-computers before now. But he'd never faced anyone so completely mean as Quint and his pals – three nasty adults armed with hunting rifles and bad attitude. There was only one thing to do. He would have to bluff it out.

'Er... I'll make you a deal,' he said.

'What are you doing, Luke?' whispered Yuri. 'You can't bargain with him!'

'If you promise not to hurt any of the animals out here,' said Luke, ignoring Yuri, 'then we'll go back and get you some help. You'll freeze if we don't.'

'Well, what a gentleman!' said Quint. 'What a kind young man!' The three men all roared with laughter. Suddenly, Quint became deadly serious. 'But I've got a better idea,' he hissed, getting close enough for Luke to smell his bad breath. 'Me and my pals are going to take that jeep, and you three can walk.'

'Then we'll freeze to death,' cried Yasmin, eyes wide and unbelieving.

'Yes, at this temperature we'll have... less than an hour!' yelled Yuri.

'So you'd better get a move on,' Quint called out as the men climbed into the vehicle. Yasmin ran over to the car and started banging on the door, but the men

just laughed through the window. They gunned the engine and zoomed off. The children watched in dismay as the hover-jeep drove away. Above them the sky seemed to darken and a cold gust of wind blew into their faces.

'Less than an hour?' asked Yasmin, turning to Yuri. 'Are you sure?'

'It could be a lot less,' said Yuri, shrugging. 'But Chung will realise we're still out here when they arrive without us in the hover-jeep... won't she?'

'She might not,' said Luke. 'We stole the hover-jeep, remember? And I don't think the security cameras were working. So nobody knows where we are.'

Milly had hidden while Quint was about, but now she was yip-yipping and jumping up and down. For a second Luke thought she might be trying to tell him something,

but then she dashed off into the snow, disappearing quickly.

'Well, at least Milly will be safe,' said Yuri. His lips were turning blue.

'We have to move,' said Luke. The three children started walking into the freezing cold wind. The snow seemed to suck at their feet and Luke's legs were soon aching. The blizzard was really blowing now and they couldn't see more than a few metres ahead. Luke realised pretty quickly they had no way of knowing if they were even going in the right direction.

Then he felt the ground start to shake.

CHAPTER EIGHT
BIG MOMMA

'Oh no, n-n-not again...' stammered Yasmin, shivering with the cold. They looked at each other as the shaking grew more intense, a deep rumbling noise drowning the sound of the storm. A ridge appeared in the snow and swiftly travelled towards them. There was no time to get out of the way before the ice beneath their feet seemed to jump, throwing the three of them to the ground.

A giant worm burst from the ground, sending a huge fountain of snow into the air and trumpeting like a thousand elephants all at once. Another one followed, then

another and another, until eight of the immense creatures formed a circle round the friends and towered over them. The worms bellowed and moaned and moved their heads from side to side, their mouths gaping wide.

'Well, it's been nice knowing you guys,' said Yuri. 'Mind you, this is pretty amazing. I never imagined I might end up as a snack for a giant alien worm.'

'And I bet the poor creatures never imagined they'd end up eating raw geek,' said Yasmin. 'They'll probably take one bite and spit you straight out again.'

'Relax, you two,' said Luke. 'I think they would have eaten us by now if that's what they wanted to do. It's not like we could do anything about it.'

Suddenly a small shape climbed down from the back of one of the worms and

came dashing towards the children. A small shape that made yip-yip noises.

'MILLY!' they cried out together. They were delighted to see her, but Milly seemed beside herself with joy at seeing them. She jumped into Luke's arms and licked his face, her long, green tongue rasping over his cheeks and nose.

'I don't mean to interrupt...' said Yasmin. The worm Milly had climbed off was bowing down, laying its body flat on the snow with its immense mouth close to Luke. Milly threw herself from his arms and clambered up onto its back again. She stood, looking at the children and yip-yipping.

'She's trying to tell us something,' murmured Luke, and then he grinned. 'Listen, I might be completely crazy, but it looks like we're going to be saved. I think the worm Milly is standing on is her mum,

and she's offering us a ride.'

'That's a bit of a stretch, Luke,' said Yuri. 'I mean, where's your evidence?'

'Oh, be quiet, Yuri, and give me a leg up,' said Yasmin. 'You can stay here and freeze to death if you like, but I'm willing to take my chance with Milly.'

Yuri scowled at her, but did as he was told. The giant worm's hide was rough, but surprisingly easy to climb. In no time at all the friends were sitting on the creature's back, Milly on Luke's lap.

'OK, how do we tell Big Momma here where we want to go?' said Yasmin.

'I suppose we could try getting Milly to do it for us,' said Luke. He stroked the little alien and looked into her eyes. 'Er... could you ask your mum to take us back to the research station? We'd like to catch up with the nasty men, too.'

Milly did a lot more yip-yipping, and they felt the giant worm beginning to move, slowly at first, but soon gathering speed. The other worms followed, and soon the children were at the head of a great column of giant worms racing across the snowy wastes, the wind and snow streaming into their faces. They had to hold on tight, but

Luke knew they were having the time of their lives.

'Now this is what I call real fun!' he yelled. 'Is this totally cool or what?'

'And I don't even care that it's freezing cold!' shrieked Yasmin, laughing.

'Hey, I can see the research station already!' shouted Yuri. 'And there's the hover-jeep. At this speed we'll overtake them before they make it back...'

And that was exactly what happened. Luke pointed out the hover-jeep to Milly, and she yip-yipped to her mum. Seconds later the worms forced the hover-jeep to stop and surrounded it. The doors opened and Quint and his pals emerged looking terrified of the giant worms looming over them. Then Quint scowled and tried to pull himself together. He raised his rifle, his hands shaking.

'Bad idea, Quint,' said Luke, tutting and shaking his head. 'I think you and your pals should drop the guns before the worms get cross.'

Right on cue, Milly's mum opened her mouth wide and trumpeted, sounding like ten thousand elephants this time, the others quickly joining in. Quint, Leon and

Biff dropped their rifles and ran screaming towards the research station.

'Ha, look at them run!' laughed Luke. 'If they think Milly's family are scary, just wait till I tell my mum what they did. They'll find out what real terror is!'

'Well, there you go, boys,' said Yasmin. 'That proves it once and for all.'

'What are you talking about, Yasmin?' said Yuri, looking puzzled.

Luke thought she was going to say that what had happened proved it was always better to be nice to other creatures than nasty. But she didn't.

'It proves... that no one in the galaxy should ever mess with us!' she said.

Luke laughed. He had to admit, she was right.